CW01642462

Michael M Roe

Tall Tales from Afar

Michael Terence Publishing

First published in paperback by
Michael Terence Publishing in 2021
www.mtp.agency

ISBN 9781800942356

To my son, Mark

Contents

Foreword

I am now retired but travel has always played an important part in my life having worked in twenty countries across the globe.

When traveling with my work, I had many unusual experiences meeting people I would otherwise never have known and learning a great deal about other cultures and peoples.

The book contains nineteen short stories and the hope is that they will entertain and surprise. The stories have unexpected endings, some of which are humorous, whereas others highlight cultural differences or some surprise happening.

Tall Tales from Afar is intended as a light read in which the reader can pick up and put down the book at any moment whether waiting for an appointment, travelling, on holiday, in bed or in hospital.

I also hope that it might make an unusual gift for someone who likes to read.

If these stories amuse and even bring a smile, I will have achieved my objective.

I have written one other book, *Tall Tales for Travellers*, published in 2008 by AuthorHouse, USA. In 2009, the book received 20 five-star ratings on Amazon.

– Michael M Roe –

(mmroe@hotmail.com)

"To travel is to discover everyone is wrong about other countries."

– *Aldous Huxley*

"Travel makes one modest, you see what a tiny place you occupy in the world."

– *Gustave Flaubert*

"Like all travellers, I have seen more than I remember and remember less than I have seen."

– *Benjamin Disraeli*

1:
An Eventful Flight

Bob and Jan were in their late twenties and had been married for three years. They lived in Los Angeles and were the parents of a six-month-old baby.

The marriage was confrontational in style and after three years the gilt was losing its shine. Bob worked for a venture capital company and was always under pressure and Jan, prior to her marriage, had been an advertising executive. Initially, she longed to give up work but was now beginning to miss not having a career. She was a bit dizzy by nature, disorganized and bored by domesticity. She had not expected that becoming the mother of a young baby would be so stressful. She found it particularly difficult being housebound and missed the social interaction of the work place.

The tensions mounted as Bob frequently returned late from work and they could not afford to go out as often as before. He was also feeling financially stretched in meeting the mortgage payments and paying off the household contents which had been purchased by credit card. These restrictions gave rise to further stress.

***

Jan realized she needed to break this burdensome routine and decided a visit to her parents would be the solution. It was difficult as her parents lived far away. They were retired military and had decided to spend their retirement in Honolulu, a location much favoured by the military for its excellent PX and Commissary facilities. She was unhappy that her parents were so far away but believed now would be a good moment to show off the baby who they had yet to see, except in photos and via Skype.

Jan approached Bob on the subject of going to Honolulu to see her parents and his first reaction was to row with his wife, saying she knew full well they were having financial difficulties and he could not afford the fare and other expenses. Later, when he had cooled down, he began to take into account that her absence for a while would be good for both of them as it would release the tension and he would be free to concentrate on his job without the stresses when he arrived back home at the end of the day.

Bob came back from work a few days later and to Jan's surprise produced a return ticket to Honolulu and a cheque for a $1,000 as spending money. She was of course thrilled and, three weeks later, having taken the baby to the doctor for inoculations, they left for a month's stay with her parents who in turn were excited at this surprise visit. Bob took the morning off to accompany them to Los Angeles Airport where they boarded a Hawaiian Airlines flight to Honolulu.

***

The flight time to Honolulu is five hours and twenty minutes and the plane was packed with holiday makers and returning retirees. Jan's seat was forward of the economy class in front of the bulk head where there was provision for a crib and more room, which made it easier to care for a small child. Jan settled in as best she could.

After about an hour into the flight, the baby began to cry. At first it was thought, as might be expected of a baby experiencing its first flight that this was due to the change in air pressure. However, as the flight progressed the crying was not just a tantrum but more serious and, at one point, the baby appeared to be turning blue. Jan was at a loss; she had only brought one extra nappy, had forgotten the wipes and the formula milk. She was getting nervous and the situation was upsetting the other passengers.

In desperation, she called for the hostess and asked if she had experienced this situation before and what was she to do. The hostess was young and inexperienced and was unable to help in a meaningful way, but said she would talk to the pilot.

The pilot, an approachable, jovial extrovert, was very experienced but for once was at a loss as to know how to react. He pointed out that he could not make an emergency landing as the flight was over water. He thought for a moment and, realizing the seriousness of the situation, decided to inform the passengers over the Tannoy system that there was an emergency concerning one of the passengers and that he was going to take the unusual measure of lowering the altitude to relieve cabin pressure.

Some ten minutes later, the baby seemed less stressed and in the absence of formula milk Jan breastfed the baby despite being without milk on the recommendation of a doctor who was also travelling on the plane. There was much relief throughout the cabin when the baby eventually fell asleep.

The plane finally landed at Honolulu International Airport and the passengers proceeded in the normal way to the arrivals area.

***

The pilot was concerned that the troubled baby had arrived without serious problems and decided to wait in the hall to meet the mother and baby. He eventually identified Jan and, on approaching, he asked:

"I hope you and your baby are alright after your troubled flight?"

"Yes, thank you for looking out for us and enquiring how we are, the baby has recovered and I am looking forward to seeing my parents who are waiting outside to meet us."

"I am pleased about that and wish you a happy stay but, before you go, may I ask how you managed to settle the baby?"

"On the advice of another passenger, a doctor, I was advised to breastfeed him."

The pilot, a serious and experienced professional was not only doing his job by showing concern but, as a sophisticated and intelligent human being and with a sense of humour, could not resist going on to add:

"Hmm, how interesting, I wish I had known about that long ago as in moments of stress over the last thirty years I have had no alternative but to chew gum."

2:
A Difficult Negotiation

Gulf Air, the airline based in Bahrain, was originally established in 1947 under the name of Gulf Aviation with BOAC (the former British airline) as the majority shareholder. In 1973, however, the regional governments of Bahrain, Abu Dhabi, Dubai and Oman took over and each state acquired a 25% stake.

Under the new ownership, Gulf Air continued to use de Havilland and Douglas DC3 aircraft but in 1977 took the decision to upgrade their fleet and buy two Boeing 737-200s. This was an important development for such a small airline and Boeing's decision to send out two senior executives to negotiate and sign the contract was seen as a compliment and a privilege given the manufacturer was more accustomed to dealing with the world's major commercial airlines.

In the late 1960s, long haul jets were not yet capable of flying the same distances as today without stopovers and the Boeing executives needed to make two stopovers to travel to Bahrain. They set out from Seattle with the first stopover in New York and the second in London. The journey took two days and included an overnight stay in London. Planes from Europe to the Middle East are invariably scheduled to land at night due to the time difference.

***

On arrival at Bahrain Airport, the two executives were not only totally exhausted and jetlagged but shocked to find that even at night the temperature was in the mid-30s centigrade. They were met at the airport by the directors of Gulf Air and ushered through immigration and customs and taken to the Hilton Hotel in Manama, the capital of Bahrain.

The Bahraini directors felt greatly honoured by the arrival of these senior executives as it was rare for an internationally prestigious multinational company to visit this small and remote island country. The directors were anxious to impress their visitors and were very solicitous as to their wellbeing. They took into account the arrivals' not unexpected tiredness, suggesting they take the next day to relax and recover from the journey. They also put at their disposal a chauffeur-driven car, should they wish to tour the island.

Bahrain has a number of locations of historic interest, including examples of pre-Islamic architecture, the impressive nineteenth century Sheik Isa bin Ali House, the former capital on the adjacent island of Murraq, the pearl museum, which is a UNESCO World Heritage site and, for those more interested in modern architecture, the skyscrapers of the banking district and, not least, the Formula I racing circuit.

The Americans turned down the suggestion, saying they had come to do business and not as tourists and proposed that they start their meetings at 9.00 a.m. the next day. The Arabs were surprised at the refusal and offended at what they understood to be a lack of appreciation of their intended welcome. Hospitality to strangers is an ingrained tradition in Arab culture and it is considered important to get to know partners to generate mutual confidence before getting down to business. This cultural misunderstanding did not augur well for the negotiations.

***

At the opening meeting at 9.00 a.m. the following morning, the Bahraini negotiators introduced the Americans to the custom of taking coffee Arab style. In the Gulf countries, the custom is different from other areas of the world. The coffee is a mixture of Arabic coffee, green cardamom, cinnamon and saffron. It is very bitter and is served in small cups. The serving of this coffee is a ceremonial act of kindness and hospitality. To those accustomed to this, it is usual to drink just one cup and then to turn the cup upside down on its saucer. Until the drinker does this, the waiter will automatically refill the cup. Not unexpectedly, the Americans were unfamiliar with the custom and it was not until the third round that they noticed their hosts had long since finished. It was apparent the coffee was not to their taste but, in the interests of politeness, they had bravely continued accepting each round. At this point, the visitors did not want to delay the proceedings further and opened their files, making it evident they were ready to begin the meeting.

It was very apparent that the visitors, not surprisingly, had yet to recover from their journey and were not at their most alert. Concentration was proving difficult and they were having a problem coping with the unaccustomed heat.

In deference to the visitors' wish, lunch was taken round the negotiating table and Arabic food was served. The meal, not unlike the coffee, was not to the visitors' taste and this added to their discomfort. The offering was a typical Bahraini lunch, and to all Arabs, the most important "ingredient" of any meal is always courtesy and hospitality, no matter how upset they might be by their guests. The Gulf Air directors had ordered what they hoped would be dishes their American guests would find interesting and had not experienced previously.

The hors d' oeuvre consisted of "*humus*" accompanied by unleavened bread, followed by a '*Byrani'* as a main course consisting of heavily seasoned rice with grilled lamb and tomatoes and a side dish of okra. As a sweet, they were served, '*gainat*', fried yeast dumplings in a saffron syrup with sugar and lemon. To drink, they were offered '*laban*' which is a salty buttermilk, not unlike seasoned yogurt. The Americans had difficulty enjoying the food but out of politeness complimented their hosts on the unfamiliar and interesting cuisine.

The Americans were also surprised that their Arab hosts were proving tough negotiators and appeared more distant and formal than the previous day when they were met at the airport. The change in manner did not appear to be the result of cultural differences and it was only then that they began to query whether they had offended their hosts.

Eventually, exhaustion as a result of the jetlag, the strange customs, the heat and hunger weakened their resolve, forcing them to alter their negotiating position and thereby accelerate a conclusion to enable them to return early to Seattle. The concessions included a guarantee to supply spare parts for a five year period and the provision of resident engineers for on-going maintenance of the aircraft. These concessions were important to Gulf Air as it would secure not only substantial operational savings but generate confidence in the airline.

***

The modernised airline now provided great prestige to the island state as it was the first regionally owned hub and became an important stop-over for international airlines travelling between

Europe and the Far East.

From Boeing's perspective, the negotiating executives considered the concessions justified and a success as the company was keen to break into the Middle East market and to beat off the competition from its main European rivals.

On their return to Seattle, the co-directors appreciated that the sale had secured a footing in a growing and potentially profitable market but were somewhat surprised at the need for the discount. The Final Sales report seemed to brush over these details and, while this was duly noted by the other directors, they never discovered the real reason. If they had, the executives might not have had received the appreciation they believed they merited given the difficult conditions.

The contract agreed for the purchase of the two Boeings was at several million dollars less than the original quotation.

After the conclusion of the deal and the exchange of the usual courtesies, they took their leave and took the next plane to London on the first leg of their journey back to Seattle.

***

On the return journey they pondered for some time as to why the negotiations had proved so difficult and particularly why it had been so hot in the conference room. They had not realized the extent to which their hosts had been upset by their aggressive stance.

As a negotiating ploy in response to the Boeing negotiators' perceived affront, the Bahraini directors had arranged for the air conditioning to be turned off.

3:
An Acquired Taste

A recently retired Danish couple were on their first visit to Australia at the suggestion of some old friends who had long since emigrated there. The couple's plan was to base themselves in Sydney so as to spend part of the time with these friends and from there make visits to Melbourne and Tasmania.

Despite the late night arrival, their friends were there to meet them at the airport and, after the embarrassment of not immediately recognizing each other after nearly twenty years, they were driven to a service apartment at Milsons Point overlooking the harbour. After a celebratory bottle of wine the friends left, conscious that the new arrivals were exhausted and jet lagged after their long flight from Europe, but not before explaining that just outside the building was a ferry stop which would take them across the harbour to the centre of the city. They were of course tired but the next morning, unable to sleep, decided to get up early and take the ferry as suggested to Circular Quay, the ferry terminal on the other side of Sydney Harbour and close to the city centre.

***

It was eight in the morning when they took the lift to the ground floor and found that the ferry station was right next to the building. It was a lovely warm morning and they waited for the arrival of the ferry. They were fascinated to observe that the ferry was the perfect tourist attraction but soon realized that to the local inhabitants it was just another means of transport, much the same as the underground in London but much more glamorous. The commuters were smartly dressed in business suits, reading their newspapers and, not unlike Londoners, carrying rolled umbrellas and briefcases. If they had so wished, they would not have appeared out of place on the London underground.

During their first few days in Sydney, they made a point of seeing the principal sights of this great city. They first visited the Sydney Harbour Bridge and took the tour over the highest point from which there is a magnificent scenic view of the surrounding area. They also went to Bondi Beach to watch the surfers, to Taronga Zoo and took a ferry from Darling Harbour to Manly, which diagonally crosses the bay.

As tourists and opera enthusiasts, they were especially interested to visit the iconic Sydney Opera House, which was designed by the controversial Danish architect Jorn Oberg Utzon.

They first went to the opera and at the same time arranged to take the guided tour round the building the following day.

The night at the opera was a pleasing and interesting experience, particularly as they had the opportunity to hear *La Traviata* sung by Joan Sutherland, the internationally celebrated Australian opera singer. Not only did they enjoy the performance but, being staid and conservative old world Europeans, were surprised and taken aback by the informality of dress and the audience's noisy reception when Joan Sutherland first appeared on the stage to cheers and clapping and to someone shouting "our Joannie".

The following day, as planned, they took the guided tour round the opera house. The tour guide was a young apprentice opera singer, very aware of his good looks, arrogant and not a little patronizing. The party was made up of the Danes and just one other middle-aged couple, thereby permitting lively exchanges with the guide without the problem of having to strain to listen to a guide as when there is a large following. The guide's exaggerated theatrical manner amused the listeners who exchanged smiles as his performance added to the occasion.

At end of the tour, which included a visit to the top of the building from which it was possible to appreciate another magnificent view to the other side of the harbour, the guide somewhat condescendingly asked the tourists if they had any further questions.

Given that the architect of the Sydney Opera House was a Dane, the building was of special interest to the Danish couple and the husband engaged the guide in a lengthy discussion about its design, the technical difficulties and the well-publicized problems in dealing with the fractious architect. At one point, the project was nearly abandoned by the government due to controversy over the design, the lengthy delays and cost overruns. The press reviews were unfavourable, the value of the enterprise questioned and the public upset by what seemed an unnecessary extravagance and misuse of public funds.

On the conclusion of the tour, the guide appeared to be relieved as he was having difficulties answering the questions and feared being caught out by his ignorance and lack of preparedness. The husband, no doubt sensing the young man's hesitation and irritated by the arrogance and haughtiness, had one last question.

"What do Australians think of the Opera House?"

The young man paused for a moment and then replied:

"We have learnt to love the Opera House as we know it is so admired by you foreigners."

4:
The Penance

Mezzogiorno, the southern half of Italy, has a long and rich history which goes back to ancient times. It is a mountainous region peppered with arid plains. Today, in many people's minds, it is infamous for its association with the mafia and a backward economy in relation to the modern industrialized northern half of the country.

While the above is true, other aspects of the region are often overlooked. Many of the isolated hilltop towns remain impoverished, but in the lowland plains there are numerous *latifundias* of up to 1,000 hectares of citrus plantations, olive groves and wheat-producing areas that account for 25% of the regional economy, the other important activity being tourism.

On one of these huge 1,000 hectare-sized *latifundias* lived Giovanni, a poor, semi-literate farm-hand. He was 22 and lived with his widowed mother in a modest outhouse provided by his employer. The dwelling was without running water and electricity. His mother worked as a washerwoman and between them they earned sufficient to meet the necessities of their humble existence. Despite their poverty, they were not unhappy as they knew no other way. Their main distractions were periodic visits to the nearby town some five kilometres away to shop for essentials and to attend church on Sundays and holy days.

Giovanni had just one friend in the village, who was ten years his senior, married with a young family and in many respects his mentor. He too worked on the *latifundium* and, being older, was better informed about the ways of the world. Their discussions were mainly about everyday life and work but occasionally they were earthier, with Giovanni's friend asking him about his interest in the opposite sex. Giovanni was very innocent about these matters and was dominated by his mother's devoutness and often did not understand that his friend was teasing him over his innocence.

Occasionally, his mother would remind Giovanni to go to confession so as to always be in a state of grace in the event of some fatal accident. He heeded this advice as he had been brought up to fear the wrath of God. He did not really understand the mysteries of the faith but never thought to question the beliefs and was always respectful of men in holy orders to whom he had been brought up to be deferential.

Giovanni, as might be expected, was not very organized and only went to confession reluctantly when coerced by his mother. On these occasions, he would take the afternoon off and walk to town. This was invariably mid-week when nobody would be in the church, except for Fr Ignacio.

On this occasion, he shyly approached the priest and explained he needed to go to confession. Fr Ignacio knew him well as a result of his regular church attendance in the company of his mother and was aware of her dominant influence over her son and his naivety and ignorance of the world in general.

Fr Ignacio invited Giovanni to enter the confessional and the priest soon followed, entering through the other side of the dividing grill. The curtains on both sides were then drawn in an effort to preserve confidentiality and privacy.

"How are you, Giovanni? I am pleased to see you in the church seeking to confess your sins. I hope you are continuing to pray."

"Yes, Father, I pray regularly with my mother and thank God for our blessings."

"Well, dear boy, what do you have to confess?"

"I have been listening to my friend's dirty jokes and have been feeling guilty."

"And so you should be, smut is offensive to God. What else do you have to repent?"

"I stole a neighbour's chicken and lied to my mother about where I got it from."

"That is serious and you must now find a way to return the chicken."

"Father, I am sorry for my sins but I cannot do that as we have eaten the chicken."

Fr Ignacio smiled to himself, unseen from the other side of the grill.

"Oh dear, but seeing as you are remorseful, I will grant you absolution for your sins in the name of the Lord."

The priest then pronounced the penance, which was three Hail Marys and a donation of twenty euros to the first lady Giovanni encountered on the steps of the church. Giovanni was upset by the need to pay the donation and would have preferred to have been given more Hail Marys, especially as he did not know how to explain the expense to his mother. However, he remembered his mother's insistence on respect for the priesthood and resolved to do as he was instructed in order to be absolved of his sins.

As he descended the steps on leaving the church, the first lady he saw happened to be standing at what appeared to be a bus stop right in front of the steps. He approached her somewhat shyly and tried to engage her in conversation. After a clumsy effort at civility, he explained he would like to give her twenty euros. The lady, to say the least, was dumbstruck and refused to accept the money. In order to convince her, he explained that the priest had required him to make this payment as part of his penance following his confession.

After this explanation, the lady enquired:

"By chance, was the priest Fr Ignacio?"

"Yes, do you know Fr Ignacio and why do you ask?"

"I normally charge 30 euros," the lady explained.

Still not fully understanding the explanation, Giovanni asked:

"Why then did the priest only ask me to donate twenty?"

"Oh, that is easily explained. He receives a discount as he is a regular customer."

5:
A Persian Pilgrim

A young man named David broke a leg while playing rugby and was taken by ambulance to the nearest hospital in London where he remained for a week under observation. A Persian nurse named Anita was assigned to look after him. He was so taken by her that on leaving hospital he invited her out and after several months proposed and they subsequently married.

Anita was of course keen that David should know her family and, at the first opportunity, they travelled to Teheran to meet her parents. David had never been to Iran and was excited at the prospect of meeting her family as well as getting to know the country.

At the time of the visit, Iran was ruled by the Shah and was very different from how it is perceived by Western politicians and the media. This remains true despite the country now being a theocracy under the rule of Mullahs. It is also to be noted that, the present regime notwithstanding, Iran is unlike any other part of the Middle East. For a start, Persians are Indo-European and not Semitic as are Arabs and Jews. The language is *Farsi* and not *Arabic*, and in ancient times Persia was an important route on the Silk Road from China to Europe. The capital, Teheran, is a bustling modern city and is a polyglot society. The Persians make up the majority of the population but there have always been Jewish, Christian, Turkish, Armenian, Kurdish, Azerbaijani, Arab and Baluchi communities. Westerners are frequently surprised when a synagogue or church is pointed out and forget that Islam is not a nation, as frequently imagined, and that Iran includes a number of communities from the non-Muslim world.

The religion of Persia was formally Zoroastrianism but since the time of the Safavid dynasty (1503-1736), the Shia Sect of Islam has been the official religion and is practised by the majority of modern Iranians. Nevertheless, elements of Zoroastrianism still remain. Zoroastrianism has its origin 3,500 years B.C., long before the existence of Judaism, Christianity and Islam and, interestingly, is the first known religion to worship a single deity, *Ahura Mazda* (Lord of Wisdom). Academic studies have confirmed that Zoroastrianism was the precursor to all monotheistic religions. The religion is now only practised in isolated areas of modern-day Iran and in parts of India, but a number of traditions still remain to this day, a prime example of which is *Norooz*, the Iranian New Year, celebrated at the time of the spring equinox.

The significance of these differences is to highlight the ethnic, linguistic, historic and cultural differences with other nations of the Middle East.

***

During the month that David and Anita were in Teheran, they were entertained lavishly by her family. On one occasion there was a reception in their honour and uncles, aunts and cousins not based in Teheran came from different parts of the country to meet this new *farangi* member of the family ("*farangi*" meaning foreigner in *Farsi*). The family was very cosmopolitan and a number of them had studied abroad, where they had met their partners. The family included a German and a Spaniard and there was much interest that it had now gained another foreign member. Anita's mother even joked she wished for a Japanese addition to the family.

When David and Anita's visit was coming to a close, there was still a brother to meet who worked in Meshed. Anita's family suggested they go to Meshed and visit him. The travel agent, however, could not confirm a return reservation as all return flights were fully booked. This was of concern as they needed to be back in Teheran within three days for their return flight to London. Nevertheless, it was decided that they would take a chance and the one-way one-hour flight to Meshed was confirmed.

Meshed is in the North East of Iran with a population of nearly three million and is Iran's second city. Its growth and importance are due to its historic past as part of the Silk Road and as a cultural and educational centre and, most importantly, the home of the Tomb of Imam Reza. This shrine is the third most important in Islam and is visited annually by eight million pilgrims.

The visit to Meshed coincided with the pilgrim season and the return problem was further compounded by a dispute between Iran and Saudi Arabia, which had temporarily banned Iranians from making the pilgrimage to Mecca. This explained why the travel agent had been unable to confirm a return flight. Anita's brother was concerned about their getting to Teheran in time for the journey to London. Appreciating the urgency, he did his utmost to find a solution and finally came up with the idea of returning to Teheran by train. The only possibility was to travel third class as advanced booking was not required, as was the case with first and second class. Given the circumstances, the brother's suggestion was accepted.

When the moment came, David and Anita climbed into an old Yugoslavian railway carriage with wooden seats and prepared for the ten-hour overnight journey to Teheran. The fare for the 890-kilometre journey was the equivalent of $5.

The train was overcrowded, with returning pilgrims already preparing to sleep on the floor of the corridor. Eventually, Anita identified an empty seat in one of the compartments and quickly claimed it. David followed and soon realized that he too would have to sleep on the floor of the compartment between the legs of the other passengers. The heat and smell were stifling. Eventually, the train set off. There were nine passengers in the compartment, four on each side with David stretched out on the floor.

The other passengers were very humble, and almost certainly illiterate, and were travelling to Teheran on their way home, having completed their pilgrimages. They came from remote parts of the country and, once in Teheran, would take a bus to their final destination. Their luggage consisted of knotted linen bundles plus portable paraffin stoves to make tea.

The passengers already in the compartment were curious to find a smartly dressed lady among their midst and shyly enquired how Anita came to be there. David was fortunate to have a *farsi* speaking wife able to give a running commentary as they recounted their stories to while away the night.

After initial introductions and a plenty of *tarof* (a ritual exchange of courtesies essential in Iranian culture, especially on meeting someone for the first time) they were astounded to find that the man lying on the floor between their legs was a *farangi*. They had never met one before. When Anita explained he was from England, they did not understand and, to avoid a misunderstanding, she informed them he was from *farangistan* (foreign lands), which they then understood. Once empathy had been established, they insisted on sharing their food which they produced from their linen bundles. The offerings consisted of a white cheese, *sangat* (unleavened bread), dried fruit and pistachio nuts, accompanied by sweet tea brewed on one of their portable stoves, served in small unwashed glass cups. Anita made it very clear to David that he was to *tarof* his appreciation, which he did in sign language. He hoped they understood. In return, Anita shared a large bar of chocolate the like of which they had never tasted. They in turn gave a long *tarof*.

At this point, instead of trying to sleep, each passenger wanted to tell their story. David was hot, bothered and uncomfortable lying between the sweaty feet but again was instructed to pay attention and on no account to fall asleep.

***

The first to tell his tale was Arash. He was forty five but looked much older and worked as a labourer at an oil depot outside Ahwaz in southern Iran, a city 820 kilometres from Teheran and requiring a nine-and-a-half-hour bus journey. He had a wife who lived in a village some distance from Ahwaz and had four sons that he had not seen in a long time but was proud that one of them had joined the army. Arash had saved for years to make this pilgrimage to Meshed, which he considered the high point of his life and claimed he was now ready to die and go to Paradise. Although it might be imagined that he had had a lonely life, he conveyed the impression that he was content. He lived on his own in a shack without water and electricity and seemed to have no interest outside the demands of his religion.

David was struck by his self-sufficiency, the simplicity of his life and lack of wants. He also wondered why he had no apparent need for family support. David concluded that his sense of peace and fulfilment was due to his limited education, lack of exposure to the outside world and the humility inculcated through his religious beliefs. Instead of being saddened by his story, David came to realize that Arash considered his life was complete and was perhaps happier than most westerners.

***

The second storyteller was Forood. Forood had been a shepherd from Qashqi and was slim with a weather-beaten face. He came from a nomadic family but had married outside the tribe and decided to settle down in one location. He worked for a large land owner. He lived with his wife and grown-up son and, unlike Arash, had an interest in his surroundings and was able to adapt to change. He had tried working in a factory to better his wage but missed the open expanses. He was musical and played the flute and, despite being a devout Muslim, was disapproving of the demands of the mullahs. He said he preferred to communicate with Allah alone. He had no shame in being illiterate and believed life's experience had provided the education he needed. He showed interest in things outside his daily life and attributed this to having left his tribe and settled down to urban life. When not at work, he liked to watch television, which he considered his window on the world, and spend time drinking tea and playing backgammon with his male friends.

***

Although by now it was well into the night and four of the nine passengers had managed to fall asleep, there was yet a third story, which was recounted by an elderly lady named Manizheh.

Manizheh had had a difficult life. She came from a village near Zahedan in Baluchistan Province close to the border with Pakistan. Zahedan is 1,400 kilometres from Teheran, is a desert area and one of the poorest regions in Iran.

Manizheh explained she had given birth to seven children and, shortly after giving birth to the seventh, her husband had died. She was destitute and dependent upon the support of the other villagers who, despite their own poverty, rallied round to help with food and care of the children.

One evening, as it was getting dark, the villagers heard a strange noise approaching across the dunes and the whole village came out to see what it was. Manizheh described what she saw as being like a camel with large eyes. It was in fact a 4x4 pickup with two *farangis* from the American Red Cross. Once the excitement of their presence had died down, one of the Americans who spoke *Farsi* asked to speak to the head of the village. The American explained that they had come to speak with a certain Manizheh as they had heard she had recently become a widow and given birth to a seventh child. The head of the village escorted them to her adobe home and the *Farsi*-speaking American spoke as follows:

"We have heard of your distress and would like to help. We have learnt that you are unable to support your family and have come to propose that the American Red Cross arrange for the adoption of your new born. The child will of course be provided for and introduced to a childless family seeking to adopt."

Initially, Manizheh had difficulty understanding the implications but was advised by the head of the village that these were well intentioned people, genuinely wanting to help. He encouraged her to accept. The Americans stayed in the village for two days, sleeping in their pickup to give Manizheh time. In the end, she agreed and, with the help of the head of the village, the necessary papers were prepared. The Americans then left with the child and went directly to the nearby town of Zahedan where provision was made for the care of the child before being taken to Teheran.

In telling her story, Manizheh unabashedly admitted that she was relieved and was thereafter better able to deal with bringing up of the other children until they were old enough to help and support her. To this day, she had no idea how the American Red Cross knew about her situation, but this pilgrimage to Meshed to the Shrine of Imam Reza was to thank Allah for the blessings she believed she had received.

Thirty years later, when her children had left home, she felt free to return the support she had received from the other villagers by helping in the fields and with the animals. Life was less stressful but always difficult.

***

Visitors to the village were rare and on one occasion a stranger arrived in a truck and somewhat surprisingly was unable to speak *farsi.* With the help of a piece paper written in *farsi,* he was able to convey that he wanted to meet Manizheh Said.

For some reason, the villagers thought he was behaving strangely and queried why a *farangi,* unable to communicate in their language, was visiting the village. With difficulty he made it known that Manizheh was his mother. The response was mixed as the villagers had difficulty coming to terms with an event that had taken place some thirty years ago and Manizheh, as a frail old lady, could not sum up great emotion for, although she realized this man was her son, the passing of time, old age, cultural and language differences made communication impossible.

Later, she came to know that her son was greatly upset by events that he had been planning most of his adult life and, as a result, only stayed a few days, during which time he bought her the largest house in the village, leaving her with enough money for all her future needs. Manizheh also learnt that her son had been adopted by a middle-class family in Virginia, had done well academically and was now a Professor of Economics at Georgetown University.

***

When the train finally reached Teheran, David was exhausted through lack of sleep, visibly shaken by this extraordinary story and overcome emotionally at how Manizheh had been able to come to terms with her situation.

On arrival in Teheran, the weary passengers gathered their belongings and climbed down onto the platform. The three storytellers set off together bound for the bus terminal where they would part company to go to their different destinations. Before setting off, they expressed their appreciation for having met and hoped one day they would meet again in Paradise.

Arash, Forood and Manizheh were very different but seemed to share the same stoicism and inner peace. How different this culture was to their counterparts in the West. Instead of egoism, ambition, materialism and righteousness, they seemed better able to accept life's hardships with a sense of spirituality born of an old culture and an understanding of not being able to counter fate.

This unexpected experience made a deep impression on David and on returning home and picking up on his daily life of commuting, suburban domesticity and middle-class financial preoccupations of mortgage and other regular monthly payments, he felt he had changed. Whereas previously, like many middle-class professionals, he was driven by the necessity to achieve and by ambition, he was finding his daily routine more difficult and having doubts about his way of life. This subconsciously played on his mind to the point it was affecting his performance at work. After dwelling on the distraction for some time he was finally able to dismiss it, realizing as a Westerner he was fantasizing about a culture which was not his own and that he should delight in his own in which he was fortunate to belong.

Three years later, on leaving his office in London, a foreigner stopped him in the street and asked him in broken English if he had ever been to Iran. Astounded by the approach and the unexpected question, he stuttered a reply that he had. The man explained he was in London to visit a brother who ran an oriental carpet business. Still reeling from the approach, David asked why he had stopped him in the street. The stranger replied:

"My name is Forood and I remember you from the time we met on the train travelling from Meshed to Teheran."

6:
A Ghostly Experience

In the west of England in the county of Somerset there is a village which, in medieval times, was a town and the centre of the wool trade. It is now considered remote, with a much reduced population consisting of farmers and small tourist hotels, which attract those interested in its history, rural ambiance, 18th century cottages and Norman history.

***

One of the main points of interest is The Manor House, which is one of the reasons tourists come to visit this out-of-the-way location. The Manor House was built in 1232 as a monastery, but three centuries later it became a baronial home on the dissolution of the monasteries by Henry VIII. The first owner after the monks were expelled was Sir William Sharington, who was granted the property by Henry VIII in 1539.

The Manor House reflects architectural development in the Middle Ages and is of great historic interest as the original Norman structure is little altered. After ceasing to be a monastery, the nave became the dining hall and the altar and sacristy, a large open fireplace which, it is to be assumed, was used to cook for the Lord of the Manor and his henchmen. At the other end of the nave, a stone spiral staircase survives, leading to the choir gallery, which was altered and extended to give access to living quarters.

To this day the large medieval structure is privately owned and modern facilities were first introduced by the Talbot family in the early part of the twentieth century. This family owned the property until after World War II when they could no longer afford the upkeep and sold the estate to a wealthy American family. This family invested further in modernizing the facilities and transformed the ancient monastic orchards and vegetable gardens into decorative grounds.

***

I came to know about this baronial manor as I was asked to "house sit" while the American owners were on an extended trip back to the United States. They had furnished the property with expensive antiques and were concerned that someone should be seen to be living there during their absence. They employed a housekeeper and a gardener, but they were only present during the day. It was agreed that while I was there no one would be allowed access other than the housekeeper and the gardener.

Despite the modernization, the atmosphere was austere and sombre. The interior stone walls and flagstone floors, high ceilings and mullion panes in tall, semicircular Gothic arches lacked the warmth and intimacy of a modern home. Worst of all, in the great hall, which was now the living room, the atmosphere was not helped by Sir William Sharington being buried under a flagstone in one of the alcoves, ironically below a small table on which the telephone now resided.

I stayed for a month minding this gloomy and oppressive property with its eerie sense of a long past era. The time passed slowly as I could not leave when the employees left having finished their work. During the day, I spent much of the time in the kitchen talking to them and drinking coffee round the kitchen table. They were local people and there was very little they did not know about the manor. I was told many fascinating tales, one of which was the long-held view among the local community that the house was haunted. They teasingly warned me not to be frightened and I laughed with them.

During my stay, I frequently pondered why anyone would want to make this a home, even a second home. At no stage did I feel comfortable. The attractions were probably seen as the beauty of the location with its quaint and historic surroundings and the dubious privilege of being Lord of the Manor. This honorific title dates from feudal times, is not inheritable and has no legal status. The privileges are limited to certain fishing rights and the flying of one's own pennant.

***

One cold and windy night when it was time to go to bed, I climbed the stone spiral staircase, walked along the corridor and entered my room. I was cold, there was no central heating and I quickly changed and jumped under the duvet. I fell asleep but in the middle of the night I was woken by occasional knocks. I tried to ignore them but, in the darkness, I have to admit I was shaken and my imagination ran riot. I did not sleep for the rest of the night.

The next day, I was pleased to see the housekeeper and the gardener and we again sat round the kitchen table to drink coffee. The housekeeper teasingly said she thought I looked tired and enquired whether I had slept well. I explained what happened during the night and they both burst out laughing. The gardener explained the flagpole was loose in its socket and when there was a strong wind it rattled. I felt very foolish.

So much for ghosts!

7:
The Magic Carpet

The much-travelled Mervyn Oram now found himself working in Kabul, the capital of Afghanistan. At the time, the country was still trying to resolve the problem of the Taliban insurgency, whose ubiquitous and often unseen presence was causing such misery and uncertainty.

The country was so war-torn by the previous lengthy conflict with the Russians that the government no longer had the capability nor the resources to repel this new threat. The Taliban were not only a worry to the government but also to the international community. It was at this point in 2001 that NATO decided to form ISAF (The International Security Assistance Force), made up of US and UK forces together with 26 other nations. These forces subsequently remained in Afghanistan until 2014.

It was 2001 when Mervyn Oram arrived in Kabul and the situation was very tense. The local people were extremely poor and much of the city was in ruins. Tanks patrolled the streets and foreign workers were advised not to visit certain areas. Foreign workers were also instructed not to take public transport and were invariably taken to their place of work by private bus or chauffeur-driven car.

In the 1970s, prior to the Russian invasion and the subsequent Taliban insurgency, Kabul was an attractive city with a prosperous middle class. However, at the time when Mervyn was working there, life was very different. There were few local amenities open to foreigners and social life was limited to restaurants in controlled areas and visits to the now internationally known Chicken Street.

Chicken Street is a narrow pot-holed street about 300 metres long with dilapidated and poorly maintained two-storey shops selling antique weapons, bronze knick-knacks, lapis lazuli, other semi-precious stones and oriental rugs. The name goes back to long before the Russian invasion when there was a well-known chicken market that formed a local landmark. With the arrival of ISAF, this street was frequented by foreign troops and workers looking to buy souvenirs. Chicken Street became jokingly known as Kabul's answer to New York's Fifth Avenue and London's Oxford Street.

Mervyn and a colleague, Kieron, lived in the same compound and shared an interest in oriental carpets. On Fridays, the Muslim equivalent to Christianity's Sunday, they liked to visit the oriental carpet shops in Chicken Street. Over a period of several months a friendship was struck up with one particular merchant with whom they had already had dealings. Mervyn and Kieron were not connoisseurs but had more than just a passing interest. It was apparent that the owner wanted to respond to their interest and on visits frequently asked them to join him over a glass of sweet tea from a samovar that was permanently on the brew. The premises were stacked from floor to ceiling with a large variety of rugs and many interesting features were explained by the merchant. On learning that Mervyn's and Kieron's contracts would shortly end and they would be leaving Afghanistan, he invited them to the back of his store. The back of the shop was how one might imagine an Aladdin's cave with a labyrinth of niches and, on reaching the furthest area, the owner showed them his finest selection, which included carpets from other producing countries, including Iran, which is acknowledged as the finest producer, with a two-thousand-year tradition of hand-woven of rugs and carpets.

Kieron was particularly interested in nomadic tribal rugs made on portable looms, the great feature of which is the use of natural dyes, whereas Mervyn enjoyed the more closely woven carpets produced on larger stationary looms based in the towns and cities.

An Iranian all silk Qum carpet caught Mervyn's eye as he already owned a similar silk carpet. The condition was poor but he was aware that, if professionally treated, it could be restored as new. He enquired as to the price and was told he could buy it for a thousand dollars. He tried to bargain, but soon realized to expect to win against an oriental bazaar merchant was an exercise in futility. He agreed to buy the carpet at full price.

On conclusion of the transaction, he enquired of the merchant how he came to acquire the carpet, given that it was not from Afghanistan. The merchant explained that the mullahs in Iran had introduced strict exchange control and that the export of rugs and carpets was prohibited. An Iran Air pilot had smuggled it out of Iran by hiding it under the pilot's seat.

Mervyn left the shop with the carpet under his arm and, when the adrenalin subsided, wondered if he had not been too impulsive. In due course, he returned to the UK and sent the carpet to a specialist for cleaning and valuation. About a week later, the expert suggested he visit him to see the result. The cleaned carpet was restored to a condition that surpassed Mervyn's expectations. The merchant valued the carpet at $15,000.

Everyone had profited from each exchange: the Iran Air pilot obtained his foreign currency; the Afghan merchant made a profit; and, Mervyn had a capital gain which exceeded his wildest expectations.

8:
Panama Shortbread

Adam was twenty-eight and had trained as an agricultural engineer specializing in irrigation. He had obtained his qualifications from the Royal Agriculture University in the UK. On graduation he worked for three years for a large commercial farm to gain experience and also to escape the hum-drum life of a small family farm.

After three years with the commercial farm, he decided to expand his experience and eventually, much to his surprise and delight, was offered a two-year assignment by the FAO (the agriculture arm of the UN) to work on an irrigation project in Panama. This he viewed with excitement and a certain amount of apprehension having previously only travelled abroad to France as a teenager on a school excursion.

On arrival in Panama, he booked into the Executive Hotel in the centre of the capital on the recommendation of his predecessor, also an agricultural engineer, whose contract was coming to an end. Despite the generous living allowances that went with his contract, Adam found living on his own in a hotel was not a long-term option and within the first month moved to a small rented apartment where he hoped to stay for the duration of his contract.

After a few weeks acclimatizing to his new assignment a work colleague, noting that he was friendly and sociable but lacking in connections, suggested he join the Panama Bridge Club which met weekly at the Paitilla Hotel and was frequented by Panamanians and expatriates. Adam followed-up on the suggestion and attended weekly where he met Carlos, a Panamanian of about the same age. They soon developed a friendship and Adam was invited to Carlos's home for dinner and to meet his mother.

Carlos's mother was a widow and Carlos her only child. She was a very gracious lady and since the death of her husband was missing her previous life, which had been very sociable. She enjoyed entertaining and was pleased to entertain Carlos's friend. Adam's first visit was deemed a great success and having observed the growing bond between her son and Adam turned the dinner into a weekly occasion. Adam not only looked forward to these evenings but was beginning to feel settled and to enjoy life in Panama.

After six months, Adam was entitled to two weeks' holiday and decided to return to the UK to visit his parents. On his last evening at Carlos's home, Adam discreetly asked him what he thought his mother might like as a present. Carlos's mother was busy preparing the meal but overheard the conversation and on returning to the dining room very forcibly insisted that she appreciated the gesture but on no account was Adam to waste his money on a gift.

Adam had no intention of returning to Panama without a gift despite the admonishment from Carlos's mother and he thought long and hard as to what to buy, concluding it had to be something British and preferably consumable so as not to upset Carlos's mother's implied wish not to be given anything permanent. He eventually decided on a popular tourist item. He knew that at tourist locations around the UK there was invariably a tourist shop and on visiting one of these locations he spotted a decorated tin box with a Grenadier guard standing on guard outside Buckingham Palace. The tin contained the popular and well-known Walker's Scottish Shortbread. He deemed this gift met his criteria: namely, something very British, consumable and generally appreciated by foreigners to the UK.

As is so often with Europeans there was the unconscious thought that as a member of the so-called developed world the gift would be introducing an element of luxury and extravagance that people from the developing world would not be acquainted with.

On returning to Panama and visiting Carlos's home for the renewed weekly dinners prepared by his mother, Adam presented his gift. On being handed the decoratively wrapped parcel, Carlos's mother gave a wry smile before opening the parcel. The lady was very appreciative and gracious and Adam felt smug that despite his inexperience in buying something for an elderly lady he had chosen well and was pleased he had not purchased an unwanted souvenir or knick-knack.

A short while later and a few days before Christmas, Adam decided to make a visit to his local supermarket. The shop was full of seasonal fare with many items from different parts of the world. These included cold meats from Poland and Germany, cheeses from France, Italy, Spain and Portugal, beers from Holland, Belgium and the Czech Republic, malt whiskies from Scotland and of course Christmas trees and frozen turkeys imported from the United States. Adam was amazed to find such a wide range of luxury items and could not help but observe the choice was wider than at his local supermarket back home. Also among the shelves was a range of biscuits and well-known international brands such as Oreos from America, McVitie's Digestives from the UK, chocolate *eclaires* and *petit fours* from France and other sweet delights from Switzerland and Belgium and, to his surprise and embarrassment, the same brand of Scottish shortbread that he had bought for Carlos's mother.

Many of these luxury items which he would have found difficult to encounter in a supermarket back home were available because of the expectations of the prosperous and growing Panamanian middle class, Panama's rapid economic development and the fact that the country was now a polyglot society of different cultures and peoples from across the globe.

Disappointed, remembering Carlos's mother's courteous appreciation which at the time he thought was her delight at receiving something with which she would not normally be acquainted, Adam continued down the supermarket aisle. As he reached the end of the aisle he came across the same Scottish shortbread stacked from floor to ceiling on offer at a discount.

He left the supermarket embarrassed by his earlier presumptuousness and humbled by his ignorance at previously having considered all non-Western countries an impoverished third world.

From this experience he began to appreciate, unlike most people from Europe, that there was a wider world than the inward looking and patronizing attitude inculcated by traditional eurocentric values.

9:
The Sting

Valleymous is a small volcanic island measuring just over forty square miles, located in the eastern Caribbean and before its devastation as a result of Hurricane Hugo in 1989 and the earthquake in 1995 was little known except as an exclusive retirement location mainly for wealthy North Americans.

To the retirees the attractions were its remoteness, historic past, lush vegetation, attractive small Georgian capital, friendly population and quiet environment surrounded by tropical woods.

The feature that distinguished Valleymous from the majority of the other Caribbean islands was that it was volcanic and did not have golden sandy beaches and therefore had little appeal to the mass tourist market.

For these reasons, the island became the private getaway for some of the richest and most prominent families from the United States, who as "snowbirds" would arrive in September in private planes with three or four months' supply of steaks and other deemed necessities not always available from the local stores.

However, it was only a matter of time before such a discreet location became known to discerning international crooks, fraudulent bankers, money launderers, drug traffickers, arms dealers and tax dodgers wishing to hide assets from their governments and in some cases from their wives.

These activities were made possible as the Valleymous government sought to generate extra revenue by trying to create an offshore banking and financial centre. In reality, the local politicians and lawyers saw it as an opportunity to line their pockets and were as corrupt as the fly-by-night fraudsters. Laws and regulations were introduced, but the absence of professional financial regulators and the lack of serious commitment on the part of the politicians meant the project was inevitably destined to end in disaster.

As the financial scandals became known internationally, foreign governments and authorities from around the globe were alarmed at the rate of expansion and the bad publicity. Also, as the island, a former British colony and now a Dependent Territory, was receiving bad press internationally, Her Majesty's Government decided as result of international pressure, especially from the US, to send out an adviser to assess the situation and close down the banks.

The person selected was Mervyn Oram, who had previously worked for various financial institutions in a number of developing countries. He was new to the Caribbean and had never previously worked as a government official. It was now that he became poacher turned gamekeeper. While responsible for the regulatory and supervisory aspects of the licensed institutions he was helped by a seconded detective from Scotland Yard to pursue the owners of those entities that were identified as acting fraudulently.

The above is by way of background and to set the scene. The scandals involved many unusual activities, but one of the most surprising was when the British Governor of the island telephoned Mervyn Oram to go to the airport and report to the Head of Customs.

Mervyn Oram drove immediately to the airport on the other side of the island and was somewhat surprised at the welcome from the Head of Customs. He was concerned that a couple had arrived in a private plane and on discovering half a million dollars in notes in a briefcase had not known how to proceed. As instructed, Mervyn telephoned the Governor informing him of his arrival at the airport and the details of his meeting with the Head of Customs. The Governor then instructed Mervyn as follows:

- Separate the couple, lock the man in the airport prison and the girl in the VIP lounge.
- Interview the man, take notes and threaten him with confiscation of the money, the impounding of the aircraft and the seizure of his passport.
- Pressure him and telephone me on the hour every hour until I say stop.

Mervyn took copious notes as instructed and was somewhat daunted by the task as he had no experience in this type of interview. The situation was not made any easier as the prison was below the control tower where there was no air conditioning nor fan. Both parties were perspiring profusely, not only from the heat but from the stress of the situation. The prisoner was visibly distraught and the interviewer not much better off.

The whole process started at about eleven in the morning with Mervyn duly telephoning the Governor on the hour. This charade continued until four in the afternoon when Mervyn was instructed to return the briefcase with the money, reunite the man with his girlfriend and hand back the ignition key to the plane and wave them goodbye.

Mervyn was confused and not a little angry at having been made to look a fool. After waving the couple off from the tarmac, at which moment the man was overcome with relief and gratitude, Mervyn drove to Government House in high dudgeon to seek an explanation from the Governor.

On arriving at Government House the Governor, in a jocular manner, congratulated Mervyn on a fine job. Without an explanation this did not go down well and did nothing to soothe his anger.

The Governor ordered tea and then explained what was happening. In the morning he had received a call from a US enforcement agency notifying him that the couple was headed for Valleymous in a private plane and asked that they be detained on the island until they had time to place an agent on each island a full-tank distance from Valleymous.

The Governor then went on to explain that when he instructed Mervyn to continue interviewing the prisoner, he did not know how long the enforcement agency would need.

The Governor had now learnt that the couple had landed in San Juan in Puerto Rico and the man had been arrested. Mervyn asked about the girl, who was extremely attractive. The Governor smiled as he had heard that Mervyn had tried to flirt with her. Mervyn blushed and denied the accusation but could not resist asking why he thought he knew.

The Governor replied that when speaking to the agency in Puerto Rico, they informed him the girl was one of their own and a CIA plant.

10:
Getting Home

A couple of friends from Sonora near the Mexican border decided to engage a young farmhand to deliver a package to a small town across the Mexican frontier with southern Arizona. It was a private transaction and not a sophisticated drug cartel operation although the individuals were members of a cartel.

Driving through the arid countryside, the two friends came across Jose, a young man walking along the side of the road. Jose was a poor and illiterate farmhand and had only ever known the small poverty stricken *pueblo* where he had been brought up by his mother and elder siblings. He made few demands and his needs were few.

The friends stopped the car and asked if he would like a lift home. He was pleased to accept. During the ten-minute ride the two men seated in the front of the car asked him if he would like to earn some extra cash. Jose's first thoughts were the needs of his family, for as far as he was concerned, money had never really featured in his life. He asked what he would have to do and how much he would be given. The passenger in the front seat then explained it would require a short journey but that it would not cost him anything. Indeed, not only would his costs be paid but he would be given $200 on his return the next day. This seemed a lot to him as he had never known such a sum. He accepted and was told that the following morning he should meet up with a friend who would wait for him outside the general store in the *pueblo*. He agreed.

The next day he met the contact and was driven some twenty minutes to a remote out of the way farm. There he was given a meal and a change of clothes and informed that he would be given a bus ticket and the necessary documents to cross the Mexican/American border. In the unlikely event his documents were queried, he was to explain he was a seasonal fruit picker. In this part of the Mexican/American border the two sides shared many long-standing cultural, family and business connections and crossings by both sides were a daily occurrence. The American side was of course sensitive to illegal crossings but given the interdependence of the communities, the crossing tended to be less strict than in other parts of the frontier. For the Mexicans, there were work opportunities and family connections, and for the Americans it was easier for the covert import of drugs.

Late that afternoon Jose was driven to the bus station and provided with the bus ticket, the necessary documents to cross the border and a small rucksack which he was to hand over to Alberto who would meet him when he arrived at his destination. The bus journey took three hours including a half-hour delay while the passengers passed through immigration control. As anticipated by Jose's sponsors, his documents did not arouse suspicion and he was cleared like the other passengers without any problem.

After successfully crossing the border, the bus continued on its journey to the nearby town, which was Jose's destination. At the bus stop, he was met by Alberto who took delivery of the rucksack and took him to a small hut at the back of a gas station where there was a bed. Jose was told he could sleep there and that Alberto would meet him in the morning to escort him back to the bus that would take him home.

The next morning, Jose walked to the front of the gas station and asked to speak to Alberto. None of the employees had ever heard of Alberto and they were surprised to learn that Jose had used their rest area to spend the night. The employees realized immediately what this was all about and suggested Jose wait for the arrival of the boss who would know what to do.

The owner arrived later that morning and the situation was explained to him. He understood the circumstances immediately and noted Jose's distress. He explained this was not the first time he had heard of an innocent young man being duped by organized crime. He also made it clear he would like to help but the only practical support he could provide would be a little cash, as to report him to the authorities or provide other help might implicate him as an accomplice. He gave Jose twenty dollars and told him he must leave and, if he could not get home on his own, he would have no alternative but to go to the authorities, which might involve his arrest as an illegal immigrant with all the problems and delays this would entail. Jose left still more distressed by his situation but appreciative of the owner's help and advice.

He left the gas station and wandered round the town while he thought about what he should do. He decided to go to the municipality and ask for advice. The man at the desk was recovering from a *siesta* and when he heard Jose's story just laughed. He had never heard such a story and in his drowsy state told him there was nothing the municipality could do and he should leave. It was now getting late. He continued strolling round the town until he came across the police station. He entered to find no one there. Puzzled, he sat on a bench outside and waited for someone to arrive. While waiting he spotted a police car in the compound and in his desperation he decided that if he could not get help, he would help himself. He knew how to drive a tractor and so he made up his mind to steal the car and drive towards the frontier. There was nobody in sight and so he broke a window, climbed in and quickly drove off.

He drove for an hour and was about to arrive at the frontier when the car stalled. He thought there might be something he could fix and decided to look under the bonnet. As he was doing so, a police car stopped and two policemen got out brandishing guns. They approached Jose and demanded to know how he came to be driving a stolen police car. Jose broke down while explaining what had happened to him and that his only intention was to get back to his home in Mexico. The more senior of the two policemen explained he was in serious trouble and would be charged as an illegal immigrant and for stealing and damaging a police car. At this point Jose could do nothing, and he was handcuffed and put in the back seat of the car. However, before setting off, one of the policemen looked over the stolen car to see why it had stalled. It had run out of gas!

On arriving back at the same police station where he had stolen the car, Jose was given something to eat and was locked up in a cell for the night.

The next morning, he was taken to the court. On hearing the details the judge could not resist a smile. It appeared he had some understanding for the young man's plight, recognizing that as a poor and uneducated farm labourer he had been duped by criminals into delivering the rucksack. He reprimanded the young man for being so easily deceived but reserved his wrath for the policemen. He demanded to know why the policemen had left the police station unattended and with open access.

The judge commented that he was more accustomed to dealing

with illegal immigrants wanting to stay in the United States than those more interested in returning to their home country.

To the policemen's surprise, he ordered them to drive the young man to the frontier and to report back that Jose had successfully crossed back into the Mexico. Failure to comply would result in their being reported to their seniors and charged with derelict of duty.

11:
The Learning Curve

John was a young man, recently married and working in a bank in the City of London. It was his first job and he planned to make banking his career. Although he had had a university education and thought he merited better, he was, rightly, made to start at the bottom and worked for two years as a clerk.

At the time he began work at the bank, computers and other sophisticated electronic equipment were still in their infancy and much of the work still required clerks to do routine tasks manually, such as book-keeping and filing. John found the work laborious and tedious and wondered whether he had made the right career choice. In the absence of equipment, which today is taken for granted, adding and subtracting was either done with a hand-held mechanical calculator or, in the case of multiplication and division, occasionally with the aid of a slide rule. On one occasion, his immediate superior complained that John took too long to add a column of figures and suggested, when the bank closed its doors at the end of the day, he visit the banking hall and ask for Mr Mitchell, an elderly clerk who had been with the bank and doing the same job for over twenty years. Mr Mitchell could sum the day's ledger entries by running a pencil down the column in less time than it took to enter the figures in a calculator. It was very impressive but made John feel inadequate and he wondered if this was an essential part of his training and whether he would ever escape being a clerk.

John thought of resigning on several occasions but was hesitant, having only recently married, and was conscious that he had never pretended to his wife that he had a prestigious position. He was feeling foolish about his inadequacy as a clerk and about the risk of losing face with his spouse. As a result, he decided to stick to the job and for two years he was moved from department to department as a continuation of his training. During this time, he became very downhearted.

At the end of two years of training, he was expecting to be given what he considered a "proper" job for which he thought he was qualified as a university graduate. This did not materialize and so he started looking at advertisements and submitting his curriculum vitae to head-hunting firms. After several weeks answering newspaper advertisements, he unexpectedly received a telephone call from a head hunter. He was invited to an interview. He of course accepted and to his surprise learnt that the job required a young man to join a little-known international firm in Lima, Peru and his application was of interest because of his apparent training from a well-known bank. Somewhat surprised that it involved an overseas position, which he had not previously considered, he waited for the outcome of the interview, which would gave him time to think over this unexpected turn of events and consult with his wife.

After several weeks, by which time he assumed he had not been selected, he received a telephone call offering the position in Peru and a few days later a contract through the post. The contract was for two years with a salary and benefits beyond his wildest expectations on condition he was able to start within the next two months. His wife, Janet, was enthusiastic about escaping suburbia and starting a new life overseas. Encouraged by Janet's response, he accepted the terms, resigned from the bank and began preparing to leave the UK. This involved visits to a doctor for vaccinations, to the Peruvian Embassy for visas and a work permit, and the buying of a new wardrobe. Both John and Janet were excited and decided, among the goodbyes to friends and relations, to learn to play bridge. They attended a six-week evening course at the London School of Bridge.

***

After arriving in Lima and starting his new job and, with help from his employer, being able to purchase a car, John and Janet decided they were now ready to socialize and joined the American Community Bridge Club as a way of making contacts. They were welcomed and informed that a new duplicate bridge competition would shortly be commencing, and they were invited to participate. It would, however, require a commitment to meet every week for three months as the tournament involved twenty tables and forty pairs. They accepted enthusiastically.

***

To those who are not familiar with this card game, it is necessary to briefly explain the need for the three months' commitment with reference to this particular story. Two factors need explaining.

Firstly, there are basically two ways to play the game, Rubber Bridge, which is the more frequently played, and Duplicate Bridge, which tends to attract the more serious players. The cards in both forms are played in the same way but the difference lies in the bidding, one of the most significant and challenging aspects of the game.

Secondly, the usual bidding conventions are known as ACOL and Standard American. They are very different but both require strict adherence as their purpose is to standardize the bidding process so all parties understand any subsequent agreement. It is particularly important in duplicate given every pair during the course of a competition plays identical hands, allowing the results to be compared. It is this competitive aspect that tends to attract the more serious players who can enjoy their imagined intellectual superiority and, on occasions, indulge in criticism of their partner or the opposing pair when mistakes are made.

***

With regard to this particular tournament, the explanation for weekly commitment over a three-month period was due to the impossibility for forty teams to play all the hands in fewer sessions.

John and Janet having learnt their bridge in the UK had only ever played Rubber Bridge using ACOL, whereas the members of the American Society Bridge Club played duplicate using the Standard American bidding system.

On the first day, the participants were invited early for drinks and for the introduction of new members. As two of the few non-Americans, John and Janet were made especially welcome and received a lot of attention. They were also pleased to find everyone spoke English as they had yet to learn Spanish. Among the members were John's boss and his wife. John and Janet were a little overwhelmed but appreciated the reception.

When the tournament began, John and Janet's first opposing pair were a middle-aged husband and wife team. The husband was a professor on loan from a US institution to a local university. He had been in Peru for just six months and made it abundantly clear to those obliged to listen that he was not enjoying the experience. He was very serious and more than a little aloof. Just prior to bidding the first hand, he remarked:

"I assume of course you play Standard American?"

To which John replied, unaware of the significance of the question: "No, we play the ACOL system."

The professor refrained from being offensive but it was apparent from his silence he was not amused. At the end of this first round, he and his wife had to move to the next table, as required by the duplicate rotation system. John began to register he was not only on a hiding to nothing but about to make a monumental fool of himself. He started to doubt the wisdom of joining this competition and became especially aware that he and Janet had committed to stay the course.

The word had already circulated that the young couple from the UK did not know what they were doing. The humiliation increased as the evening went on.

At one point they were inevitably paired against John's boss and his wife. Like all the other rounds, John and Janet lost badly and they soon realized they were a source of amusement and the butt of jokes. On leaving the table his boss remarked:

"I trust you did not put bridge on your curriculum vitae as one of your accomplishments."

As the evening continued, there was humiliation after humiliation and the other players looked forward to beating them and gaining easy points. John and Janet had not only become nervous but very embarrassed at their inexperience and naivety in thinking that because they had been to a bridge school they were ready to participate in a tournament.

***

On many occasions during the three months they thought about quitting. The tournament Director made it clear that this would upset the functioning of the rotation system and would not go down well with the club members. They also sought to find a replacement, but this was also unacceptable as their results would not be a fair reflection of a team's performance.

Finally, the competition came to an end. There was much relief on the part of John and Janet that the ordeal was over. However, before making the obligatory farewells, they were approached by the Director:

"We all understand that you are no doubt pleased the tournament is over but I want you to know I think you have bravely tolerated a situation that must have been difficult and at times uncomfortable. Nevertheless, we count on your attendance at the black tie celebratory dinner next week."

In his heart John had no wish to attend but thought not to do so would be a further loss of face. He accepted the invitation.

***

On the appointed evening, John and Janet appeared in the dining room of the five-star hotel and were greeted with smiles. They were not comfortable but were fortunate to find a table at the back of the room with an elderly couple who had shown understanding when their turn had come to play against them.

When the dinner was over, the Director announced there would be a prize-giving and, after a short speech thanking the participants, spoke as follows:

"Before announcing the winners, I have a special request. Will John and Janet please come forward."

There was loud applause and laughter and when they arrived at the head table they were handed a decoratively wrapped present. The Director asked them to open it and show it to the members. It was a book: *How to Play Duplicate Bridge.*

12:
The Chinese Murder

Xinjiang Province is an autonomous region in the northwest of China with long borders to the north with Russia, to the east with Mongolia and smaller frontiers to the west with a number of central Asian Republics. Xinjiang is the largest of the twenty-two provinces in China with a land area of just under 10 million square kilometres. It has a long history as one of the most important routes on the ancient Silk Road.

Xinjiang's large area, distant location, remoteness from China's heartland, small population, numerous different ethnic groups and forty different languages make it difficult for both the central and provincial governments to impose their authority. The result is that there are abuses, corruption and neglect.

***

In this environment lived two childhood friends, Zhang Wei and Wang Yong, one was a cook and the other a carpenter. Their homes were in the same neighbourhood in a small town not far from Urumqi, the provincial capital.

One night, the two were smoking opium when they began a stupid argument over the culinary merits of Xinjiang over those of Shanghai. When the short-term effects of the opium had worn off, they took leave of their senses and started to fight. Under the effects of their drugged state, the fight got out of control, ending with Zhang Wei hitting Wang Yong on the head with a saucepan. Wang Yong collapsed unconscious, bleeding from the back of his head, while Zhang Wei, still drowsy as the effect of the opium wore off, fell asleep before he could fully take into account what he had done.

Wang Yong, despite his injury, was the first to regain consciousness while his erstwhile friend remained pale and unconscious, stretched out on the floor. Wang Yong, in his heightened anxiety, thought his friend was dead from an overdose and panicked. He struggled to his feet, still bleeding and, suddenly becoming aware of the enormity of what had happened, fled.

Zhang Wei took longer to recover and, although surprised not to see his friend, learnt subsequently that he had left town. On recovering from the evening, he continued with his regular daily existence until he was visited a few weeks later by the police and charged with murder. The police had discovered a headless corpse on a local rubbish dump and immediately suspected that Zhang Wei was responsible. He of course denied any connection with the corpse but the police took him into custody while they investigated. For weeks the police pursued their enquiries but found no evidence to connect Zhang Wei with the corpse. The investigation received a lot of attention in the local community and this put pressure on the police to produce a result. Anxious to obtain a confession, Zhang Wei was deprived of sleep, fed only on rice and made to run round a courtyard on a full stomach until he dropped. He was then left in solitary confinement to recover. As a poor and ignorant man, he had not known how or whether he could get help.

Despite the People's Republic of China having enacted major legal reforms in the 1970s, the People's Court at the municipal level, especially in remote areas, had yet to fully implement the new legal processes. There were few checks and balances and the police were able to use their power to ensure a conviction. Zhang Wei was sentenced to life imprisonment.

In the interim Wang Yong, on fleeing the province, imagining he had killed Zhang Wei, travelled to Shanghai in the belief that he would be less easily discovered in a large city. He found casual work washing up in the kitchen of a large restaurant and felt safe as he was not required to register with the authorities nor to produce identification documents. He worked in the kitchen for several years before deciding to risk going back to Urumqi where he was entitled to welfare benefits. On his return, it was only then that he discovered his former friend had been in prison all this time and had been accused of his murder. Wang Yong, feeling foolish at having run away for a crime he had not committed, went to the police and convinced them he was very much alive. The police had no alternative but to demand the People's Court overturn the conviction and release Zhang Wei.

Zhang Wei went home, only to find his wife had remarried and his children had been put out to adoption.

13:
The Panamanian

Latin America covers two continents, North and South America, and extends from the southern border of the USA to the southern tip of South America, and includes twenty-one countries. The languages spoken are mainly Spanish and Portuguese but there are a number of smaller pockets where English, French and Dutch are spoken. Given the vast area it is not surprising that the region has huge diversity. This diversity extends beyond geography and climate to significant differences in history, culture and economic development. This is not always appreciated by those unfamiliar with the region who, not infrequently, think of it as whole and dismiss it somewhat disparagingly.

Chile, for example, is now classed as a First World country by the IMF. Over the last twenty years it has reformed its political institutions, diversified its export economy from dependence on the volatile price of copper and has a prosperous and well-educated middle class.

Economic disparities, however, continue across a number of countries as a result of unreformed political systems, economic mismanagement and poor educational facilities. The poverty in these countries is often extreme.

To the surprise of many, Panama ranks in the upper quartile in terms of development. It is a small country with a diversified service economy and a population of just four million, of which half live in Panama City, the capital.

In addition to the Panama Canal, which links the Atlantic with the Pacific, it is home to the second largest Free Trade Zone Area (after Hong Kong), is a banking centre, a regional airline hub, a tourist and shopping centre and the regional base for eighty multinational companies.

The regional contrasts are not solely due to differences in the availability of natural resources, but also on the impact of migration of peoples of all races. Panama, despite its small size, has one of the most diverse mixes of people from anywhere in the world.

Interracial marriages are viewed as unexceptional and the acceptance of all people by the educated milieu is taken for granted whatever a person's background or ethnicity. This is not to say there are not social distinctions, but they are based more on economic status. This makes Latin America, and Panama in particular, different from other parts of the world, and is of great benefit and a feature to be admired.

***

Shortly after arriving in Panama, Adam, an agricultural consultant from Europe under contract with the Food and Agriculture Organization, was invited by one of his new colleagues to a private party. This friendly gesture was by way of introducing him to friends, appreciating that as a recent arrival in Panama he may have been feeling a bit strange and lonely. The invitation was much appreciated.

On the appointed night, Adam had difficulty finding the apartment building, as Panama City is poorly mapped and signposted. The locals find a new destination by going to a well-known local landmark then following instructions such as: once outside the landmark turn left and then second right and ask someone in the area to identify the apartment building.

On arriving at the apartment, Adam was welcomed by his host and ushered into a crowded room where there must have been twenty other guests.

During his conversations as he circulated he was interested to learn that many of the guests originated not only from Europe, North America and the Caribbean but were also from Asia in addition, of course, to the indigenous peoples. He could not help but observe how the interaction would be different in a similar situation in Europe. Whilst of course a foreign visitor would be welcome, it is likely there would be a subconscious awareness that they were from a different culture, requiring a certain formality and perhaps limiting spontaneous exchanges. What surprised Adam was that the guests, despite their different origins and cultures, considered themselves Panamanian first and not from their country of origin.

As a country boy from a family farm in the mountains of Wales, Adam, with his parochial background and preconceived ideas as a national from the developed world, suddenly became conscious of his lack of sophistication and even ignorance.

Despite these thoughts, he continued circulating and was introduced to an attractive Chinese lady of about his age. After exchanging names and the usual initial courtesies, the conversation went as follows:

"Do you like being in Panama?" Adam asked.

"Of course, I live here."

"What do you do?"

"I am a doctor."

"Do you have a specialty?"

"Yes, I am a psychiatrist."

'If I may ask, where did you study?'

"I first qualified as a medical doctor at the University of Panama."

"And subsequently?"

"I obtained a PhD from Harvard."

"Where do you practise?"

"I am a Senior Psychiatric Consultant at John Hopkins Hospital here in Panama."

Adam was impressed and not a little surprised that such a lady should be so qualified and holding a senior position at such a young age. Fascinated, he wanted to know more and continued with further questions.

"Having spent a long time studying in the US explains why you speak such fluent English."

"Thank you, but I would never have been accepted at Harvard if I had not already had reasonable proficiency in English, which I acquired as a child while at school here in Panama."

"You must also, no doubt, be an accomplished linguist, speaking Chinese, Spanish and English."

"Chinese?"

"What! You are not Chinese speaking?"

"No, we speak Spanish at home."

"How is it that you do not speak Chinese?"

"My ancestors came to Panama in the 1890s to work initially under the French and subsequently under the Americans on the construction of the Panama Canal and I am an eighth generation Panamanian."

14:
The Sisters

Mr and Mrs Dudley lived in Streatham, a middle-class suburb of London. They led a quiet life, were devout Christians, conservative in outlook, wary of foreigners and with few interests outside daily life. They had two daughters, Cynthia and Amanda.

The two girls went to the same nearby state school, were very close and supportive of one another with the same friends and interests. Surprisingly, however, they had very different personalities. Cynthia was serious and plain while Amanda was attractive and outgoing. Cynthia, now twenty, was two years older than her sister and both were starting out in life.

Cynthia, like her parents, was a devout Christian and opted to enter a nunnery. Her parents were happy at this decision, knowing she would be secure for life and pleased she would not be too far away as the nunnery was just outside London.

Amanda decided to go to secretarial college and on qualifying found employment with an Austrian import/export company. She left home and rented a small apartment in central London to be near her work which she shared with a friend from her college. Unlike her sister, she enjoyed socialising and acquired a wide circle of friends. She also developed a close relationship with her Austrian boss.

Her boss, Sacher, was in his early thirties and soon the relationship with Amanda became serious and after three years when his company needed him back in Vienna, he proposed. Much against the wishes of her parents she accepted and, despite her anxiety at distancing herself from her family and all that was familiar, she followed Sacher soon afterwards to Vienna.

Three months later Sacher and Amanda married, but much to her disappointment her parents refused to attend the wedding. They could not come to terms with the fact that she had chosen to marry a foreigner and live abroad. She felt further alienated from her past. She continued to try and keep in touch with her parents but over time they lost interest and only her sister, now lost to the world in a nunnery, remained in contact, with occasional brief exchanges on birthdays and at Christmas.

During her first three months in Vienna prior to her marriage, she stayed at a hostel for young women and took every opportunity to get to know this majestic and noble city. She was amazed by the grandeur of the Baroque architecture and the city's history as the former capital of the Hapsburg Empire. The sense of history was overwhelming. She was equally overcome by the elegant lifestyle, the operatic traditions, the classical music of Straus, Schubert and Haydn and of course the famous Viennese waltzes.

In the early days of the marriage she was introduced to Vienna's famous cafes, Viennese culinary traditions and the much celebrated Wachau Valley wine district, now a UNESCO heritage site. They were happy but it soon became apparent Sacher was a playboy and, although discreet, he neglected the marriage, despite the outward appearance of the marriage being successful.

On coming to terms with the situation, Amanda decided to

relieve her inner loneliness by accepting a position in a fashionable haute couture establishment. There she met prominent society ladies frequently accompanied by their husbands, presumably included in the outing to pay the bills. As an attractive foreign lady now speaking fluent German, she frequently caught the roving eye of the husbands who accompanied their wives.

One gentleman in particular seemed to sense her loneliness and pursued her relentlessly. She was flattered by the attention, his good looks and obvious wealth. Eventually she succumbed and became his mistress. This gave her a new sense of self-worth and independence.

In the course of time, she put her new circumstances to good use and became a successful businesswoman, eventually taking over the fashion house where she worked. Part of her success was due to her understanding of the importance of elegance and dress in Viennese society.

As a consequence of her success, she became well-known and accepted in society, receiving frequent invitations to the opera, society balls, carnivals and the long standing Viennese tradition of salons by fashionable ladies.

This pleasant and successful life carried on for several years, but suddenly it came to an abrupt end when inexplicably she started coughing, becoming fatigued and short of breath. She was referred to a leading specialist and after chest x-rays and numerous examinations was diagnosed as having contracted chronic bronchitis.

Initially, she tried to keep up with her social life but, as she weakened as the months passed, her condition deteriorated and she was eventually confined to bed. She was just fifty-nine. She had expected to be supported by her long-standing social friends, but to her disappointment they fell away as her condition worsened.

She soon realized she was approaching death and was particularly saddened that her social friends were abandoning her. As she sensed her time might be limited, she decided it was the moment to make a will.

In thinking about her will she had always wanted to remember the long-standing friendships she had made during her career and her happy times in Vienna, but was saddened to find how superficial they were now that she was unable to join them when she most needed them.

She called her lawyer and made a will. She died alone shortly afterwards accompanied only by her maid.

The lawyer published her death in the *Weiner Zeitung* and *Die Presse*, Austria's leading daily newspapers, and the funeral was held in the local Catholic church. It was attended by the maid and a small group of mainly former employees.

After due process and the granting of probate, it was revealed the sole beneficiary of her fortune was Amanda's sister, Cynthia.

Cynthia was now abbess of her convent and, overwhelmed by her sister's generosity, arranged for a commemorative plaque to be installed at its entrance. Cynthia also prayed daily for her sister's soul, encouraging the other nuns to share in gratitude for their good fortune and pleading with the Almighty that Amanda's soul rest in peace.

Amanda continued to be regularly remembered in services as a great benefactor.

Several months later, Abbess Cynthia made discreet enquiries about her sister through the British Embassy in Vienna and was shocked to learn the truth and did not now know what to do about the plaque or what to tell the other nuns. She feared somehow the truth might become known but decided to chance that it would never be revealed and to spend the rest of her life living the lie.

Amanda had been the owner of the most successful brothel in Vienna.

15:
Noblesse Oblige

Mervyn Oram was a bachelor working on a long-term contract with a bank in Bahrain and had a spoilt existence which included a car, a large villa and a servant who came each day, all of which were paid for by his employer. Each February, he used to invite his mother, Idina Oram, to stay for a month. She lived in the UK and, as a widow who lived on her own, this was the highlight of her year.

Many of Mervyn's social activities had to be curtailed while his mother was staying, but they both enjoyed each other's company and the numerous attractive amenities available in Manama, the capital.

Each year she booked a return ticket with the then Yugoslav Airlines which now no longer exists following the collapse of Yugoslavia and the breakup of the country into several independent states.

Yugoslav Airlines was a small underfunded state-owned airline. The management was poor, scheduling unreliable, the hostesses inadequately trained and the seats uncomfortable. The airline had also been on more than one occasion the subject of UN sanctions. The reason for its existence was the need of the Yugoslav Government to earn hard currency. It is also interesting that Bahrain was only a refuelling stop as part of a longer flight from London to Australia and, although a non-passenger stopover, the airline offered the occasional empty seat at a heavy discount to fill the plane. It was only through a helpful travel agent that Idina got to hear about this opportunity.

Idina was in her late 60s and, due to her reduced financial circumstances, very careful with her modest pension, putting aside a small amount each month to be able to afford the fare. She was also very stubborn and independently minded, refusing to accept her son's offer to pay for the ticket.

Mervyn of course met her on arrival at Bahrain Airport and drove her to his villa, a short distance outside the capital. The villa was in a compound with five other villas with a well-manicured garden. She was pleased to be away from the UK winter and to enjoy the warm weather, spending long periods in the grounds watching the wild birds feeding, especially the parrots who each year at this time migrated from Pakistan.

The compound also had a swimming pool and the Indian servant looked forward to Idina's visits and always made a great fuss of her, following her around the house and attending to her every need. She appreciated his well-meaning attention but at times found his presence overbearing. She liked to swim in the cool of the evening and he would pace up and down by the side of the pool holding her towel. She did not say anything for fear of offending him. She soon learnt to climb out of her bedroom window to escape his attention when she wanted to swim.

On occasions, Mervyn had to travel on business and, when this happened, the servant used to stay in the villa to take care of Idina. On one occasion in the middle of the night she needed to go to the bathroom and got up as quietly as she could so as not to wake him. Nevertheless, he heard her and when she came out of the bathroom he was standing there with her glasses on a tray. She of course thanked him but explained, as sensitively as she could, that she did not need them to do what she had to do.

The month passed quickly and the time approached when she had to return to the cold weather in the UK.

The return flight on Yugoslav Airlines was scheduled to arrive in Bahrain for refuelling on its way from Sydney to London at 1.00 a.m. Idina and Mervyn arrived at the airport at 12.00 p.m. only to be informed that there were only two seats available but three passengers with tickets. This was a little concerning as it was already late for Idina. The check-in clerk suggested she wait until the other two passengers appeared and he would then see what he could do.

The other two passengers soon arrived. They were a young American couple who had been visiting friends in Bahrain. They were informed about the overbooking and immediately suggested that Idina take one of the seats. In no uncertain terms Idina made it very clear she would not hear of it and insisted that, as a couple, it only made sense that they should take up the two seats. After a very courteous exchange and realizing that this old lady was quite adamant, they accepted her logic and when the plane landed boarded the flight.

The check-in clerk, appreciating Idina's difficult situation, asked her to wait a while and he would try and arrange something. Twenty minutes later he returned with a smile. He had explained the circumstances to a Malaysian Airline official and between them they had agreed to book her onto the airline's next flight to London, which was scheduled in an hour. At this point Idina was very appreciative and relieved to know she would be able to get home.

Malaysian Airlines is a well-established and well-regarded airline. On hearing of the situation the hostess went out of her way to escort Idina to her seat and to Idina's amazement found she was in the First Class section. When she queried this, the hostess said this was not a mistake and welcomed her aboard. She had to fight off sleep to enjoy the wonderful attention and meal.

On arrival at Heathrow Airport, she had originally planned to continue her journey home in the west of England but realized she was too tired and emotionally drained and decided to stay at the airport hotel until later in the day. She booked into a room and spent a few hours resting, after which she went to the reception area and sat down on a lounge chair and ordered a coffee to gather her wits before setting off. While relaxing over her cup of coffee she was amazed to see the young couple walk through the entrance. The young couple were equally surprised to see her, expecting her to have been delayed in Bahrain and not to have arrived before them. The young couple looked bedraggled and exhausted and explained their plane had stopped in Belgrade, the Yugoslav capital, before continuing on to London, and they were now planning to rest for a while before catching their flight to Boston later in the day.

The couple had a short chat before excusing themselves because of their need to rest. Fond farewells were exchanged and after checking in they left to go to their room. Idina then pulled herself together and went to the reception counter to request the booking of her coach ticket and to settle her bill. She proffered her credit card, hoping there were sufficient funds to meet the unplanned stay at the hotel. She waited apprehensively for the clerk to prepare the bill. He then approached and informed her there was nothing to settle. On enquiring why, she was told the bill had already been paid by the young couple who had just checked in.

Her relief was palpable and her gratitude immense at the

generosity of the young couple. She would have wished to thank them but did not know their surname and only knew that they came from Boston.

16:
The London Taxi Driver

An American entrepreneur based in Dusseldorf was working on an innovative heat pump with a German partner when they needed venture capital to advance the project. The American was advised to make contact with a merchant bank in the City of London where there were a number of institutions specializing in investing in start-up opportunities.

Through his business connections he was introduced to a London-based consultant known to be well connected with financing sources. This was in the 1970s before the world became globalized and the City still worked on the basis of the "old boy" network. The consultant to whom the American was introduced was called Jocelyn Hampton-Jones and, as part of the upper echelons of British society, had been educated at an exclusive private school and Oxford University. By virtue of this background, he had good connections to the world of private banks.

The American entrepreneur agreed to come to London and the consultant arranged to meet him at his hotel and take him to a pre-arranged meeting with a prestigious private bank. In conformity with establishment tradition, the consultant was dressed in a Savile Row suit with rolled umbrella and briefcase. On arrival at the hotel, he asked the receptionist to advise the businessman that he was waiting for him in the lobby.

It was a hot and humid afternoon when they met in the lobby

and to the consultant's horror and embarrassment the American was dressed in an open-neck floral silk shirt, light summer trousers and had a gold chain round his neck. Instead of a wallet he sported a hand-held handbag which hung from a strap on his wrist. The consultant cringed but did not know how he could explain old fashioned conservative banking dress code without giving offence. He knew immediately the meeting at the bank would be a failure but he had no choice but to go through with it. He feared for his future relationship with the bank and his reputation within the City.

As expected, the stiff upper lip bank director received this client haughtily and with exaggerated courtesy, as only the British upper class knows how. This pantomime was however lost on the American who thought his presentation had impressed and he had been well received. On leaving the bank, the consultant did not feel it was his duty to disillusion him, knowing that on his return to Dusseldorf the American would shortly receive a flowery letter thanking him for providing the bank with the opportunity to hear about his interesting proposal but regretting the bank could not pursue their interest at this time.

Not unexpectedly the consultant's worst fears were confirmed when the next day he received a curt call from the director expressing his disapproval that the consultant had not checked the background of his new client and for wanting to introduce a sponsor who was 'not one of us'.

On returning to the hotel in a taxi, the conversation was difficult, particularly as the American had no understanding of the impression he had made and felt that the banker had been appreciative of his presentation. On arrival at the entrance to the hotel, the American unzipped his handbag while still in the taxi and settled the fare. The taxi then went on its way.

On climbing the steps to the entrance to the hotel, the American suddenly let out a loud cry. The receptionist heard the cry and came to find out what was the problem. The American explained that he had left his handbag in the taxi and it contained not only his passport and return ticket to Germany but ten thousand dollars and his credit cards. The receptionist did everything she could to calm and reassure him, including offering a stiff drink. When he had recovered his composure, she told him that if he were to go to the nearest police station, it was almost certain the handbag would have been handed in.

The American was incredulous and was already wondering how he was going to get back to Germany without a ticket, passport and money. The police station was fortunately only a short distance away and he and the consultant went on foot. As they arrived, they could see the taxi driver waiting on the steps. The taxi driver in turn was upset:

"Why on earth have you taken so long? I have been losing business which I cannot afford to do."

He handed over the handbag to the American who was dumbfounded to find his passport, ticket, cash and credit cards present. He immediately gave the taxi driver a hundred-dollar bill stating this would never have happened in New York and asked why he was so honest, to which the driver replied:

"I spent two years cycling round London in all weathers studying street names and layouts to pass what is known in the taxi community as "The Knowledge" in order to obtain my taxi driver's licence. Why would I want to risk losing the licence when I have a lifetime's work ahead and a family to feed?"

17:
An Unexpected Friendship

It is probable that Mary and Penelope would never have met had it not been for World War II. Britain in the minds of many has always been associated with clearly defined class distinctions reflecting education, economic status and regional accents. While this cannot be denied, they are frequently exaggerated, a source of amusement to foreigners and the subject of music hall jokes.

The war, however, brought many changes, not least of which were social. The civilian population became affected to an extent not previously known. This was particularly true for the female population. Despite the diehard conservatism from both sides of the political divide, it was recognized that women were needed in the workplace as the men were being recruited to fight the war.

During the war women, for the first time, worked in factories where they manufactured bombs, ammunition, warplanes and other much needed military equipment. They also worked on farms and as drivers and nurses. During the course of the war up to half a million women are thought to have been employed by government and voluntary institutions such as the Land Army and the WRVS (Women's Royal Voluntary Service). It also meant they were frequently the breadwinners in the absence of the head of the family. As a consequence, the war years broke down the class structure and helped in the emancipation of women. Social relations could never revert to how they were before the war and this irreversible development was further enhanced by the egalitarian socialist government in the years immediately after peace was secured.

It is under these changed social conditions that Mary and Penelope came to meet.

***

Mary came from a working-class family in a town called Farnborough, some distance from London. She went to the local school and had little experience of the world outside her home town. At the age of twenty four when the war broke out, she decided to look for work in London. She contacted the WRVS who determined that, as a result of her experience driving her father's grocery van, she should be trained as a chauffeur for army officers based in London. This not only required training as a professional driver but also how to cope with the "blackouts" (no street or other lighting at night), the 1940 "blitz" (the German Luftwaffe bombing raids) and later from 1944 the "doodlebugs" (self-propelled bombs launched from Germany). She adapted quickly and was reputed to say several years after the war that this was the happiest time of her life. The "live now" for fear of being of bombed meant there was a communal *esprit de corps*, lots of partying and merry making. It was during this time she met an American officer and they planned to marry when the war was over. Tragically, he was killed during the Normandy invasion. She never got over the loss, never married, and until the end of her days was bitter and cantankerous, succumbing to heavy drinking.

Penelope, by contrast, came from an aristocratic family, was educated at an exclusive private school and in 1937 became a debutante and was presented at Court to King George VI. Despite these social refinements she was rebellious and, much to her parents' dismay, wilful and a social embarrassment. She decided to leave home and marry the first person who proposed. The man she accepted was a captain in the army who, shortly after their marriage, was posted to Burma. When he returned he was a changed person and rather than divorce, which at the time was difficult, they agreed to separate and he decided to work overseas. As part of an agreed separation, he purchased a long lease on favourable terms on a war damaged property in London which he assigned to Penelope. He then left for South Africa never to return. Penelope, instead of being upset, was relieved but without money of her own having been cut off from her family, she struggled financially. Further, as she had been brought up to be a "lady" in opulent surroundings she was not trained for anything and unable to find a suitable job. Friends helped her make the house habitable and she then decided to let rooms. This provided a subsistence-type existence but not what she hoped for.

Her first tenant was Mary. Mary, as earlier mentioned, was a down to earth practical sort of person and soon noticed how Penelope was like a fish out of water in her new and unaccustomed surroundings. On returning each day from work, Mary helped repair the plumbing and the laying of carpets and other household necessities while Penelope looked on helplessly. Initially, Penelope by way of contributing offered cups of tea and perhaps even a meal such as baked beans on toast (she had no idea how to cook). There was much goodwill between them and eventually, partly through friendship and understanding of each other's loneliness, a lasting friendship was established.

***

It is difficult to understand how two people from such different backgrounds could develop such a close understanding. It is only to be imagined that the war experience, disillusionment with their past, their current economic circumstances and the failure to establish a permanent relationship were the binding factors, and of course their shared belligerent and feisty natures. They were both in need of support and continuity.

The relationship, surprisingly, lasted for the rest of their lives. It was confrontational and they argued frequently, especially over money, drink and their different expectations.

As the years passed, they tired of the struggle of living in a big city and moved to a small rented cottage in a remote part of the west of England where they lived in the company of numerous pets and existed on a state-provided old age pension. It was during this time that they made a pact. Whoever became seriously ill would be looked after by the other, whatever the circumstances. It happened that Mary became terminally ill with chronic pustule psoriasis, a terrible affliction resulting in blisters covering her whole body which left her in permanent pain. She was a brave and stubborn lady who spent seven years confined to a special bed which minimized pressure on the most sensitive areas. She refused to receive visits and her only companions were two cats that slept by her side and Penelope, who did everything possible at great personal sacrifice to make her situation tolerable.

When Mary was no longer able to meet appointments at the hospital, she was visited by doctors and special carers who were astounded by her bravery and fortitude. Penelope later claimed Mary's endurance of such pain over seven years was due to her fear of the devil for being a 'rotten catholic'.

After knowing Mary during the course of her long illness and realizing she was as poor as church mouse, the doctors and the carers decided among themselves to club together for her to stay in a private hospice. The next day an ambulance came to collect her. Penelope was truly grateful for their understanding and support and was overcome with emotion and relief when Mary was taken to the hospice.

A few days later, the moment arrived, it was late at night when Penelope received a telephone call asking her to get ready as a car would come to collect her in the next few minutes. When the car arrived, she was quickly taken to the hospice.

***

The hospice was an elegant ivy-clad Georgian mansion. Outside there were manicured gardens and a nearby lake where the quacking of the ducks could be heard from the house. On entering the panelled hall, Penelope could smell the scent of the flower arrangements as she was greeted by Mary's doctor. He explained Mary's condition was now rapidly deteriorating and it was the moment to bid goodbye to her friend.

The atmosphere in the hospice was one of sombre peace but to Penelope it was joyless and depressing. She slowly climbed the oak spiral staircase and on reaching the top of the stairs was met by a stern matron dressed in a uniform with starched collar and cuffs and sensible black shoes. It reminded Penelope of the much-dreaded matron of her schooldays. The matron addressed her in sharp tones as follows:

"Your friend is in the last room on the right and I have to warn you she will not be able to hear you unless you kneel by her pillow and speak into her ear."

The corridor was long and Mary's room was at the end. When Penelope opened the door she saw her friend, not unexpectedly looking frail and wizened, remembering she once weighed nine and a half stone and was now only four and half. Despite her bravery and feistiness, her dreadful struggle over seven years had taken its toll. Penelope, as instructed, knelt by her pillow and spoke into her ear:

"Please do not worry, I will of course take care of the cats and follow all your wishes."

To which Mary, true to her feisty nature, managed to sit up and say:

"The nurse is a silly old cow, I heard every word."

She then fell back on the pillow and died.

18:
The Illegal Immigrant

Peter Albright was a British mining engineer based in Peru, working for a UK copper mining company. He had been with the company for five years and was now settled in Lima having married a Peruvian lady and planned to remain permanently in Peru.

As Marketing Manager, he was frequently required to travel abroad. On one occasion, he needed to spend a day in Panama to visit a business associate. In 1966, before long-distance commercial jets were introduced and airlines were still flying turbo-prop planes, frequent stop-overs on long distance destinations were the norm. On leaving Panama, Peter was subsequently going to have to change flights in Miami and New York to travel to London.

Whilst in Panama he chose to stay at the Riande Hotel located next to the airport as after his meeting on the day of his arrival he did not intend to return to the capital as it was some distance from the airport. The next morning he checked out of the hotel early having decided to wait for his flight in the terminal.

On presenting himself at the airline desk, he was informed that his passport had expired the day before and consequently the airline could not accept his passage. Dismayed, he telephoned the British Consulate and was advised that if there was sufficient time before his flight, he should take a taxi and come to the consulate. Fortunately, having decided to check out early from the hotel, there was just enough time.

Understanding the urgency, the consulate obligingly arranged for him to have a new passport photo and quickly completed the other formalities. Peter then rushed back to the airport in a taxi. The clerk at the check-in desk was now able to confirm that his passport was current and duly issued the boarding pass.

The flight time from Panama to Miami took six hours and, on this occasion, it was already night when the plane landed in Miami. In those days, the airport was not as modern as it is today and from the aircraft to the terminal building there was a long cement walkway covered with an awning. There were few passengers and as Peter walked along the passage he sensed footsteps close behind. He quickened his step and whoever was behind did the same. On entering the terminal building two burly uniformed men grabbed Peter by the shoulders. He was asked if his name was Peter Albright and, when he acknowledged that it was, they escorted him to a small waiting room where they took away his passport, ticket and hand luggage. Peter was informed he was an illegal entrant to the United States since he was travelling without a valid passport.

***

Peter protested vehemently that the passport had been renewed earlier the same day and that they should check this before accusing him of trying to enter the country illegally. They ignored this and dismissed the claim without checking the passport. They subsequently left the room, taking his belongings, and locked him inside.

***

Three hours later he was escorted to a plane leaving for New York. The plane was full and, on boarding the plane, he was escorted by these two burly uniformed officials to a seat at the back of the plane. His escorted appearance by these uniformed thugs caused quite a stir among the other passengers. At this point Peter was tired, hungry and more than a little concerned as he was still without his passport, ticket and other belongings.

On arrival at New York, it was early the following day and on leaving the plane two more uniformed officials were waiting for him at the foot of the aircraft and again he was shown to a waiting room and locked in. He was there for a further three hours, after which the guards took him across the tarmac in an official van to a waiting plane. Again, he was shown to a seat. He was happy to learn the plane was destined for London. Mentally and physically drained, he fell asleep, only to be woken half-way into the flight by a stewardess who returned his hand luggage and handed him a buff envelope with his documents.

This harsh, baseless and completely unwarranted treatment bothered him for some time. Eventually, he was able to dismiss the experience but has never understood how an advanced and respected country could allow these strong-arm tactics by unthinking low-grade officials to be a foreigner's first experience on entering the country.

As a senior executive in a mining company, Peter had travelled to many different remote and far-flung locations in Africa and Asia, but despite local bureaucratic shortcomings he had not experienced such treatment.

19:
The Dilemma

On leaving school at eighteen, James's father, who was working abroad, wrote to ask his son to which university he had applied to study for his degree. On learning that James had not planned nor wanted to go to university, his father wrote a letter telling him to come to his senses and not throw away the opportunity of having a serious career.

After various exchanges with his father in which James explained he wanted to be independent and earn money, his father offered to finance a year's sabbatical if, during that time, he would rethink his future and the need to acquire a degree or professional qualification.

After consulting friends from school, James learnt that a good place to go for a sabbatical year would be Grenoble University in the South East of France and to study for a diploma in French and French literature. The consensus opinion among his friends was that, not only was it an attractive city, but close to the border with the Switzerland and the Cote d'Azur with easy access to well-known skiing resorts. Furthermore, it was attractive to like-minded students from many different countries and the one-year diploma course was not too demanding.

As an adolescent of eighteen and only just out of the restricting environment of a boarding school, the distractions sounded irresistible, especially as the academic requirements did not seem too onerous.

He applied and was accepted and at the right moment travelled to Grenoble by train and cross-channel ferry to Dieppe from where he continued his journey by train. On arrival in Grenoble, he booked into a modest hotel where he intended to spend only a few days before locating cheaper lodgings. He suddenly felt free and now considered himself an adult. Like many adolescents, he thought he could cope with any situation, but during his time in Grenoble he had some unexpected and hopefully maturing experiences.

Within a few days of meeting his fellow students who, like him, were in high spirits having also escaped parental control for the first time, he was invited to a party. There were young people from all over Europe and even the United States and, after consuming more wine than he was used to, James overcame any shyness and circulated freely.

When the party was over, he staggered back to his dingy hotel room, was very ill, slept through most of the following day and woke up with a dreadful hangover. Worse still, he woke up to find his face covered in spots. Trying not to panic, he decided to go back to bed in the hope that when he woke up for the second time they would have somehow disappeared. Later that day, he was disturbed by a knock on the door. It was the landlady wondering why she had not seen him leave his room. When she saw his face she was horrified and said she would immediately call for a doctor. The doctor arrived, diagnosed chicken pox and recommended he stay in his room for at least a week, prescribing a soothing lotion and putting him on an unpalatable diet of boiled chicory which was considered appropriate as a cure.

James suddenly found himself confined to his room, in a strange environment, having nothing to do, with no one with whom he could communicate and with a disgruntled landlady obliged to follow the doctor's prescribed diet. He was at a loss as to how to cope with this unexpected situation. He became very depressed and the only diversion was a few magazines in French provided by the landlady. He soon realized he had no choice but to accept the circumstances. It was the first time he was without family support and it was a wake-up call.

While languishing in his room trying to sleep as much as he could to pass the time, his only contact with the outside world was the occasional visits of the doctor and the delivery of his meals by the landlady who would leave a tray outside the door for fear of becoming infected.

On the third day, he heard a further knock on the door. He expected the visitor to be the landlady but to his surprise it was an African American whom he had met at the party. This thoughtful gentleman explained he had been surprised not to see him in any of the lectures for the last two days and was wondering if something had occurred. On seeing James's face, he immediately understood. James was quick to explain that he had chicken pox to which his friend informed him that he had had it as a child and would not now be re-infected.

James was truly appreciative of this friend's visit and an animated conversation followed. James attributed his thoughtfulness to his maturity. He was in his early thirties and a lecturer at Wisconsin University in the United States. The friend also explained he was only in Grenoble on holiday for a short while, hoping to improve his French. While in Grenoble, he visited James daily and always brought gifts such as fruit and biscuits, and reading material, which he realized would help James pass the time. Shortly after these visits and James's recovery, the friend had to return to the United States.

When the friend was back at Wisconsin University they corresponded, but after a while this died away and the relationship drifted apart, no doubt due to the greater maturity and sophistication of the American university lecturer.

On recovering from his chicken pox, James found a small apartment which gave him his independence and, through the university, made a lot of contacts among which were a group of three French students with whom he spent much of his time.

In March there was a four-day Easter break and the three friends invited him to join them on their trip to Marseille. The agreement was that when they reached Marseille each would go their separate way. He readily accepted.

On arrival in Marseille, James decided to try and hitch-hike to Nice. It took all of the second day and it was only the following day he was able to look around. As it was March, it was cold due to the Mistral (a strong north westerly wind which occurs in the spring in Southern France and can sometimes reach over a 100 kilometres an hour).

At the end of the day, James went to buy his coach ticket that would take him the following morning back to Grenoble. As the ticket was more expensive than he had budgeted for, he realized that as the bus did not leave until 7.00 in the morning he had a problem deciding how to spend his remaining time. He deemed he had three alternatives: enjoy a good meal and then worry about how to spend the night; have a good night's sleep in a hostel and worry later about finding something to eat; or, go to the cinema and see a film round twice which would kill time and keep him warm.

After much deliberation, he decided to go to the cinema and, as luck would have it, Jacques Tati's hilarious film *Monsieur Hulot's*

Holiday was showing.

After paying for the entrance, he was now without any money until he got back to Grenoble. It was 11.30 at night when he came out of the cinema and he had to decide how he was to pass the rest of the night. He remembered being told by the travel agent that the coach terminal was at the top of the town next to the railway station. He made his way there wondering all the time how to find somewhere out of the cold.

On exploring locations and noting the coach station was indeed nearby, it occurred to him he could sneak into the railway station waiting room although the problem later would be how to escape without a ticket. He decided to take a chance.

On finding the waiting room, he was delighted to discover there was a coal fire and the room was warm and welcoming. However, all the benches, except one right at the back of the room, were occupied by fellow tramps. He immediately claimed it. No doubt it had not been occupied because of its distance from the fire. He settled down as best as he could and fell asleep exhausted.

At about two in the morning he was woken by voices. It was the Stationer Master asking the other tramps in turn what they were doing there and, dissatisfied with their answers, told they to leave. Eventually he reached James at the back of the room and he was asked the same question. By this time James had been able to observe what was happening and when approached by the Station Master was ready with an answer. He claimed that he was waiting for the train to take him to Grenoble. The Station Master hesitated in his reply and was doubtless assessing the truth but, after deliberating for a moment, said he could stay.

At six in the morning when the railway station appeared

deserted, James was able to sneak out undetected. He then made his way to the coach station. Being one of the first passengers to arrive, he selected a seat at the back of the coach so that later he could stretch out and sleep.

The coach from Nice to Grenoble can take up to seven hours as it takes the Route Napoleon across the Alps. James tried to enjoy the spectacular views but was too hungry and exhausted to appreciate the occasion. What was still more difficult was that periodically the bus stopped for the passengers to stretch their legs and buy refreshments. Given his financial circumstances, James did not leave the coach. He also tried to avoid contact with the other passenger so as not to reveal his hunger and distress.

Finally, the bus arrived in Grenoble and he rushed to the student dining hall knowing that the food, even for students, would exceed any expectations in a similar institution back home. Adding to his angst, he found the restaurant closed and would not reopen until seven, another three hours away. At this point, feeling drained and weak with hunger, he slumped onto a nearby public bench and bemoaned his misfortune.

One of the features of French cuisine is the accompaniment of bread with meals, usually a baguette, and on this occasion James ate the equivalent of a whole baguette while waiting in line to be served at the counter. Once seated, he ate a double portion of his selected meal. Finally, replete with a bloated stomach, he struggled back to his apartment. The resulting fatigue, weakness and the effects of over-indulgence lasted two days.

It is of course well-known that students stretch boundaries as part of growing up, but to this day James still wonders whether he made the best choice.

While alone in his apartment recovering for the two days, he spent time dwelling on his experiences. Initially, as a cocky, know-all adolescent, he was pleased with himself for overcoming the difficulties, not wishing to remember the anguish, hunger and pain he had gone through for his failure to plan better. But, as he gained strength, he began to realize the difficult experiences he had to overcome were not, as he imagined, confirmation of his manliness but the unplanned actions of an unthinking, even irresponsible youth who through the failure to plan had let himself down.

What would you, the reader, have decided in his situation: a full stomach, a good night's sleep or a means of passing the time?

About Michael M Roe

He started his career with a bank in the City before accepting a position with an investment company in Lima, Peru.

On leaving the company, he went on to be an emerging markets consultant with the World Bank, a UK government agency and other international agencies which led to assignments in twenty countries across the globe.

The experience generated an interest in how different customs inhibit understanding of alternative political systems, cultures and religions and encouraged him to write this book.

Michael is now retired and lives in the South West of England.

Available worldwide from Amazon

Michael Terence Publishing

www.mtp.agency

www.facebook.com/mtp.agency

@mtp_agency

Printed in Great Britain
by Amazon

68027899R00061